For Scarlet who is also very good at sharing oatmeal! ~ S S

For Sam – you know why! ~ T W

Copyright © 2011 by Good Books, Intercourse, PA 17534
International Standard Book Number: 978-1-56148-711-0
Library of Congress Catalog Card Number: 2010031620

Text copyright © Steve Smallman 2011
Illustrations copyright © Tim Warnes 2011
Original edition published in English by Little Tiger Press,
an imprint of Magi Publications, London, England, 2011

LTP/1500/0131/1010 • Printed in Singapore

Library of Congress Cataloging-in-Publication Data
Smallman, Steve.
Icky little duckling / Steve Smallman ; [illustrations] Tim Warnes.
p. cm.
Summary: Mr. Rabbit likes for everything to be neat and just so, but
when he brings home something smooth, speckly, and perfect and out pops
a very messy but affectionate duckling, he discovers what he has been missing.
ISBN 978-1-56148-711-0
[1. Orderliness--Fiction. 2. Rabbits--Fiction. 3. Ducks--Fiction.
4. Animals--Infancy--Fiction. 5. Loneliness--Fiction.]
I. Warnes, Tim, ill. II. Title.
PZ7.S639145Ick 2011
[E]--dc22
2010031620

Icky Little Duckling

Steve Smallman   Tim Warnes

Good Books

Intercourse, PA 17534, 800/762-7171, www.GoodBooks.com

Mr. Rabbit liked everything to be **just so**:
every flower, **just so**, every pebble, **just so**,
every leaf in the forest perfectly neat—
and **just so**.

One day he was busy tidying when he found
something smooth and speckly and perfect.
"Oh, my whiskers!" he gasped. "You're just
the thing for my collection!"

Mr. Rabbit hurried home. He carefully washed the perfect, speckly thing and placed it, **just so**, in the middle of his collection.

He loved it. He often sat
polishing it and humming
a happy little hum.

But then one evening—CRACK!
A jagged line appeared down the side
of Mr. Rabbit's perfect, speckly thing.

"Oh, my whiskers!"

he gasped in horror. "Don't worry!
We'll soon have you mended!"

But it was too late.

CRACK!

It broke in two...

...and out came something icky,
sticky and strange. Not **just so** at all.
It looked up at Mr. Rabbit
and said ... "**Mama!**"

"Mama!"

"**What?!**" cried Mr. Rabbit. "No, no, no, I am *not* your..."

"**Mama!**" it said again, even louder.

Then it hopped on to the floor, grabbed hold of Mr. Rabbit's leg and wouldn't let go.

"Yuck!" groaned Mr. Rabbit. He popped the icky, sticky thing into a big, bubbly bath. "First, you must be clean! We'll find your Mama in the morning."

"Quack!"

Soon there were bubbles on the floor,
bubbles on Mr. Rabbit, and bubbles
all over the burrow!
"Goodness me!" gasped
Mr. Rabbit. "You're a duckling!"

Gurgle-urgle-urgle! went the duckling's stomach.
"Oh, bother," grumbled Mr. Rabbit. "*Now* you're hungry.
Aaaaa . . . do you like oatmeal?"

The little duckling *did* like oatmeal.

She liked to sit in it…   she liked to splash in it…

and she liked to share it
with Mr. Rabbit!
"Yeeeuck!" groaned
Mr. Rabbit and filled up
the tub again.

"Mama!"

"Yawn!" went the little duckling.
"Bedtime, thank goodness!"
cried Mr. Rabbit.
"It will soon be morning!"

He popped the duckling
into a box and tucked
her in, **just so**.

"Mama?"

But the duckling didn't
stay **just so** for long…

Mr. Rabbit flopped into his chair.
"**What a mess!**" he groaned.
"I'll tidy it up in the...

zᶻZ z zᶻZz z!"

"**Mama?**" whispered the little
duckling. She scrambled on to
Mr. Rabbit's lap, snuggled up
and fell fast asleep, too.

Next morning, they set off to find the duckling's Mama.

Duckling found
a stretchy thing...

and some spotted bugs.

Then she found a grumpy old
prickly monster and had to have
a hug from Mr. Rabbit.
But they didn't find
her Mama.

Back at home, Mr. Rabbit made some more oatmeal. The duckling found lots of lovely things to play with!

"Put those down!" shouted Mr. Rabbit. "Carefully! Oh, I hope we find your Mama soon!" he sighed.

Feathers

Candles

Beach things

But they didn't find her the next day. Or the day after that.

Then one morning down beside the stream, the duckling shouted, "**Mama!**" And this time, she was right!

She leaped to meet her family in a happy huddle of kisses and quacks.

Then as Mr. Rabbit turned to leave,
the little duckling jumped into his arms and
gave him a great, big, feathery hug.

"Thank you so much, Mr. Rabbit!"
said Mrs. Duck.

Back in his burrow, Mr. Rabbit scrubbed and polished until everything was as neat as before.

His books were **just so**.
His boxes were **just so**.
And his collection was
tip-top, totally **just so**.

But he didn't feel right. Everything was
just so, but he was just so ... lonely.
Even his special things didn't
seem so special anymore.

Then Mr. Rabbit started to smile ...
"Oh, my whiskers!" he cried.
"I'll need lots of oatmeal!"

Mr. Rabbit invited the duck family for breakfast.
His burrow didn't stay neat for long, but it was filled
with giggles and quacks and fun and friends.
And Mr Rabbit thought it was **just perfect!**